First published in the United States, Great Britain, Canada, Australia, and New Zealand
in 2018 by NorthSouth Books Inc., an imprint of NordSüd Verlag AG, CH-8050 Zürich,
Switzerland.

Distributed in the United States by NorthSouth Books Inc., New York 10016.
Library of Congress Cataloging-in-Publication Data is available.
ISBN: 978-0-7358-4325-7
Printed in Latvia
1 3 5 7 9 • 10 8 6 4 2
www.northsouth.com

FSC
www.fsc.org

MIX
Paper from
responsible sources
FSC® C002795

The Little Drummer Boy

By Bernadette Watts

In a faraway town there once lived a little drummer boy called Benjamin.

Benjamin played his drum every day, in front of shops and market stalls, by the doors of houses, or in front of the inn.

Benjamin was a poor orphan. He had no home. He slept where he could, in summer under a tree, in winter in some corner between buildings away from wind and snow.

When people felt happy they danced to his lively tunes. When they felt troubled his music gave them peace. Many people were kind to the poor boy and would bring him bowls of hot soup or some bread.

Winter was coming. The mornings were frosty, but Benjamin was on the streets playing his drum every day.

The days got shorter. The moon and stars shone long before day's end.

And the brightest star in the whole night sky stood right above the town.

On one of these cold days three strangers, riding horses, came into town. They spotted the little drummer boy and rode up to him. The horses were tall and proud, saddled with tapestries and hung with bright tassels. The strangers were also richly dressed in silks and furs decorated with jewels.

One of the strangers said, "We have traveled from a distant land. That new star has guided us here, to this town, to find a newborn king. We bring him gifts. We want to honor him. . . . Come with us so you too can honor him."

The strangers gazed up at the star that shone so brightly right above the inn.

The second stranger said, "That is the place where the newborn king lies in his cradle. . . . Little drummer boy, come with us to honor him."

The strangers turned their horses toward the way that led to the inn.

But the third stranger looked back at Benjamin and said, "That's a merry tune you play. It fills my heart with joy. . . . Come with us to honor the newborn king."

"Oh no!" replied Benjamin. "I am too poor and shabby to visit a king! And I have nothing to give him."

The stranger paused for a moment, smiled kindly at the poor boy, but then turned his horse around and followed his companions.

Benjamin stared after them and wondered if they too were kings.

He shivered in the cold, jumping up and down to keep warm. But he went on playing merry tunes on his drum for the people who were hurrying home.

House doors were firmly shut against the cold wind. Then candles and lanterns were lit in the windows.

Then as it got darker, the first flakes of snow drifted down.

And then Benjamin saw some shepherds with their sheep who had walked into the town and were now crossing the marketplace. The shepherds had seen Benjamin; they knew him and so stopped to speak to him. One shepherd boy, a friend of Benjamin's, carried a lamb. He said, "Benjamin, we saw a host of angels above our fields this evening. The angels spoke to us! They told us a new king has been born . . . here in this town. We are bringing a lamb, and some fleeces, to keep him warm. The angels said to follow that big new star shining over the inn. Come with us, Benjamin, to honor him."

Benjamin shook his head sadly. "I am just a poor drummer boy, a beggar with nothing to offer a king.

"And I am so cold now so I must find some sheltered place to curl up and sleep."

One of the shepherds gave Benjamin some of the food they had carried with them.

Then, all together, the shepherds said again, "Come with us!"

But Benjamin just shook his head again.

The shepherds and the sheep and their sheepdog turned into a side street that went around the houses and into the way that lead to the inn.

The little drummer boy felt sad to see them go.

It was now getting darker and very cold. The snow had stopped falling, but the streets had frozen.

Benjamin found a place to shelter. He felt so sad and lonely.

Suddenly a girl came running along. Her clogs clattered on the frost-hard road. Her hair streamed out in the wind.

It was Rachel! Benjamin and Rachel were good friends. She worked at the inn, serving food, washing dishes, sweeping floors. She saw Benjamin and ran up to him, calling out, "Benjamin! Have you heard the news?

"A new king has been born. See that bright star right over the inn? That is where he lies!

"I am going to see him and give him these little warm shoes. Come with me!"

But Benjamin said, "Look at me in old ragged clothes. . . . I have nothing to give. . . . I cannot come."

Rachel said, "It does not matter. Look at me too! A serving girl in old clothes nobody else wants! But I must honor the newborn king. He will not look at our clothes, only into our hearts. Come with me, Benjamin . . . now!"

She then took Benjamin's hand and together they ran toward the inn.

From afar they saw the shepherd boy, still holding the little lamb. The shepherd boy called out, "Rachel! Benjamin! Come, follow me!" And he pointed to the stable, which stood in front of the inn. The stable door stood wide open, and light streamed out across the snow. The shepherd boy turned, and clutching tightly to the lamb he ran across to the stable.

One of the rich strangers and one of the older shepherds stood outside. Then they carefully went in, and the shepherd boy followed them.

The herd of sheep standing outside peeped shyly through the doorway.

Rachel and Benjamin came to the open doorway and looked in.

The three strangers knelt in the straw. The shepherds stood quietly at the back, but the young shepherd boy stepped forward and put down the lamb.

There were animals in there too; a donkey stood on one side and a big ox on the other side.

It was very peaceful inside the stable. Even the chickens were quiet.

Rachel held Benjamin's hand very tight and pulled him into the brightness and the warmth.

There in a simple crib lay a tiny baby, his mother and father on either side.

Rachel pulled Benjamin to the front.

One of the strangers whispered, "Here is our newborn king. We bow before him."

The three strangers laid gifts before the little family and then stood back.

The shepherds came quietly to the crib and put down the fleeces. The lamb lay close to the child. Then Rachel put down the tiny, warm shoes too. She smiled at the baby and the baby smiled back.

But the little drummer boy had nothing to give. He stood there feeling awkward and useless.

The child's mother looked kindly at the little drummer boy. She said nothing but only smiled.

Suddenly Benjamin said, "Shall I play my drum for the new king?"

The mother and father nodded and smiled happily.

So Benjamin played a gentle tune. . . . The baby waved his tiny hands and kicked his tiny feet.

Benjamin played on . . . lullabies and songs. . . . The baby laughed with delight.

The little drummer boy felt his heart fill with joy. He felt warm. He felt loved.

He played on and on. There was never a winter night filled with such wonder and happiness.